LIFE WITHOUT ANIMALS

WHAT IF BEAVERS DISAPPEARED?

ANTHONY ARDELY

Gareth Stevens PUBLISHING

Please visit our website, www.garethstevens.com. For a free color catalog of all our high-quality books, call toll free 1-800-542-2595 or fax 1-877-542-2596.

Library of Congress Cataloging-in-Publication Data
Names: Ardely, Anthony, author.
Title: What if beavers disappeared? / Anthony Ardely.
Description: New York : Gareth Stevens Publishing, [2023] | Series: Life without animals | Includes index.
Identifiers: LCCN 2021043911 | ISBN 9781538276204 (set) | ISBN 9781538276211 (library binding) | ISBN 9781538276198 (paperback) | ISBN 9781538276228 (ebook)
Subjects: LCSH: Beavers–Juvenile literature. | Beavers–Behavior–Juvenile literature. | Beavers–Conservation–Juvenile literature.
Classification: LCC QL737.R632 A73 2023 | DDC 599.37–dc23
LC record available at https://lccn.loc.gov/2021043911

Published in 2023 by
Gareth Stevens Publishing
111 East 14th Street, Suite 349
New York, NY 10003

Designer: Rachel Rising
Editor: Kate Mikoley

Photo credits: Cover, p. 1 Don Donelson/Shutterstock.com; pp. 3, 4, 6, 8, 10, 12, 14, 16, 18, 20, 22-24 Igor Kyrlytsya/Shutterstock.com; p. 5 Annette Shaff/Shutterstock.com; p. 7 Richard Seeley/Shutterstock.com; p. 9 Smeerjewegproducties/Shutterstock.com; p. 11 SGeneralov/Shutterstock.com; p. 13 ForestSeasons/Shutterstock.com; p. 15 Ronnie Howard/Shutterstock.com; p. 17 BMJ/Shutterstock.com; p. 19 Chase Dekker/Shutterstock.com; p. 21 Ivie Bouchard/Shutterstock.com.

Printed in the United States of America

CPSIA compliance information: Batch #CSGS23: For further information contact Gareth Stevens, New York, New York at 1-800-542-2595.

CONTENTS

Boldface words appear in the glossary.

Big Beavers

Beavers are the second-largest **rodents** in the world. In North America, they're the largest. Besides people, beavers make more changes to their **environment** than any other animal. Without beavers, our world might look pretty different!

In the Water

There are two species, or kinds, of beavers. American beavers live in North America. Eurasian beavers live in parts of Europe and Asia. Both kinds live in and around water, such as streams, rivers, or lakes.

Busy Beavers

Beavers have large, strong teeth. They use them to cut down trees! Then, they use the wood they've cut down to build a dam. The dam creates a pond. There, the beavers build their home, called a lodge.

Home Sweet Home

The ponds beavers make aren't just home for them. They're also home for many other animals, such as fish and turtles. Some birds like to land in these ponds instead of in more open bodies of water.

When beavers build dams, it raises the **water level**. Sometimes, the water floods. If people live nearby, they don't always like this. However, it helps create **wetlands**. Wetlands are an important **habitat** for many more plants and animals.

Cleaning Creatures

Bodies of water with beaver dams are often cleaner than those without them. Why? The dams slow water down. This allows dirt and **pollutants** floating in the water to sink or stay behind as the water flows away.

Problems for Beavers

Beavers were once killed off almost entirely for their fur. Today, some people view these builders as pests. They may trap and take them away from their habitat or kill them. Humans also sometimes build on land where beavers live, pushing them out.

Why We Need Beavers

By creating its own home, the beaver provides a place for many other plants and animals to live. If beavers disappeared, so would the dams, ponds, and wetlands they make. Life without beavers could mean life without many more animals.

Beaver dams may cause flooding, but they also help control it. Without beavers, there would likely be more harmful floods **downstream**. These animals help create **complex** communities of living things. Share what you know and help keep beavers safe!

GLOSSARY

complex: having to do with something with many parts that work together

downstream: in the direction of or closer to the mouth of a stream or river

environment: the natural world in which a plant or animal lives

habitat: the place or type of place where a plant or animal naturally or normally lives or grows

pollutant: something that makes something, such as water, land, or air, dirty and often not safe to use

rodent: a small, furry animal with large front teeth, such as a mouse or rat

water level: the height of the surface of a body of water

wetland: land containing high levels of moisture in the soil and usually covered with water at least part of the time

FOR MORE INFORMATION

BOOKS

Borgert-Spaniol, Megan. *Beavers: Wetland Architects.* Minneapolis, MN: Super Sandcastle, 2020.

Statts, Leo. *Beavers.* Minneapolis, MN: Launch!, 2020.

WEBSITES

Beaver

kids.nationalgeographic.com/animals/mammals/facts/beaver

Look at pictures, watch a video, and read more fun facts about beavers on this website.

Beavers

www.dkfindout.com/us/animals-and-nature/rodents/beavers/

Take a look inside a beaver habitat and read more about these animal builders on this page.

Publisher's note to educators and parents: Our editors have carefully reviewed these websites to ensure that they are suitable for students. Many websites change frequently, however, and we cannot guarantee that a site's future contents will continue to meet our high standards of quality and educational value. Be advised that students should be closely supervised whenever they access the internet.

INDEX